ALPHA

ALPHA

JEREMIAH MOSS

authorHOUSE®

AuthorHouse™
1663 Liberty Drive
Bloomington, IN 47403
www.authorhouse.com
Phone: 1-800-839-8640

Published by AuthorHouse   03/25/2013

ISBN: 978-1-4817-3021-1 (sc)
ISBN: 978-1-4817-3020-4 (e)

Library of Congress Control Number: 2013904885

CONTENTS

DEDICATION

This book is dedicated to my immediate family, especially my mom, who have provided so much love and support from the day I was born.

It is also dedicated to my godmother, Aunt Yoreel, who always sends me resources about dinosaurs so I can study the creatures that once ruled the earth.

I also give special thanks to my godmother, Aunt Bonita, who worked tirelessly editing the manuscript and helped get this book published. And lastly, I would like to thank my Uncle Mark Jones for giving me the most spectacular advice about achieving all of my dreams.

Thank you and I love each of you dearly.

Jeremiah

Pronounciation of Main Characters' Names

Usarian	—	(U-sar-ian)
Zafod	—	(Zay-fod)
Saebr	—	(Sa-ber)
Tsurok	—	(Ser-rock)
Notch	—	(Noch)
Nook	—	(N-oo-k)

PROLOGUE

People always tell stories about legends of the mighty Bigfoot and the vicious Chupakabra and all, but the one story that people have never told, is the one about a mysterious island that was populated by animals and dinosaurs. Most creatures were humans who could morph into all kinds of creatures. They were known as Morphers. This island was ruled by Kings and Queens. The frightful thing about it was that a volcano erupted every year. But magically, on the day after the impact, the island comes back to life with new plantation and new creatures. This land was called Morph Island, an unknown territory located in the Atlantic Ocean, south from Iceland.

The temperatures in the winter were so cold it would go below -10 degrees Celsius, while in the summer it would reach above 100 degrees Celsius. Luckily for the creatures, they could adapt to any season.

It was said that on the thirteenth year, the volcano would erupt for the last time, but the island would not come back to life. Instead, the island will burn in ashes and sink into the bottom of the ocean depths forever.

The island was full of competition. Usually, the King and Queen would live in a 50 ft Gorge with more than forty family members who would also fend off bitter rivals and keep the throne safe. But, if they failed to defend their territory, the King and Queen were forced to give up their throne and the enemy would take over. This meant a new King and Queen, a new family, and a whole new ball game for the island.

You see, there was only one common rule for the nature of this island, and that was: to <u>SURVIVE</u>.

CHAPTER 1

THE LAST KING

It was now the twelfth year on the island, as spring had just arrived, and there was a hatchling Prince named Alpha. He had loving parents named King Zafod and Queen Miriam and a loving family who always volunteered to babysit him and his siblings whenever their parents were absent. Before the Prince hatched, the volcano erupted killing everybody and everything on the island. The family was forced to jump in the ocean which was filled with Sea Monsters. Sadly, the entire family, including the King and Queen and his siblings didn't make it. The Prince's egg however, wasn't destroyed. On the day the island turned back to normal, flowers were in full bloom, a soft breeze was blowing in the air and other life forms roamed the island and then it happened—Alpha hatched.

As the years went by, Alpha understood that he was born without parents or a family. But, he would have dreams about them and his mother was always there to guide him throughout his life. Alpha was no longer a Prince, but at the age of eighteen, he was crowned as King of Morph Island. It was finally the thirtieth year and he was known as the Last King of the island.

Alpha had been having difficult times as the last king because unlike the past kings, he never had a family to back him up. He was pretty much fighting off enemies by himself. He also never had a Queen in his life. Alpha knew if he had to do all of this stuff solitarily, before the final eruption, he had to know every technique he could think of. So far, Alpha had been successful in keeping his crown over the years. It seemed as if no one could defeat him. But backing down was never the rivals' option and the King knew about it. He had to always be ready for another fight. Alpha would never know what other obstacles he might have to overcome; he would always be prepared.

Every day the King drew carvings in his den, showing his hunts, fights, and dreams.

CHAPTER 2

THE KING'S HUNT

Alpha had not eaten meat for weeks, relying on only plantations and fruits. Now it was time for him to go hunting. He decided to eat a duck-billed Dinosaur called a Hadrosaur, one of his favorite meals. He left his gorge and walked into the woods.

He walked for about a half mile until he had finally spotted the herd he was looking for in the open grasslands which consisted of Zebras, Buffalos, Deer, Antelopes, Kangaroos, and Elephants along with Mammoths, and Woolly Rhinos.

As he morphed into a T-Rex, licking his chops, he was detected by one of the Elephants. It sirened the herd and they ran. Alpha darted out the woods and ran after them as he looked for the weakest and the oldest Hadrosaur. He used all of his speed to catch up, but the herd led him through a bush and straight into Triceratop territory.

Alpha remembered his horrific encounters with this herd. He remembered trying to eat one of their young, but an adult suddenly used its horn and stabbed his left leg. So Alpha had always tried his best to avoid them. As the King surrendered his hunt and turned away, the herd charged, sending him running for his life.

Alpha knew he was going to eat soon. He was determined not to give up, and saw two of his favorite meals called Iguanodons. They were teenagers fighting for dominance. They made loud bellow-like noises which were heard through the whole woods. Knowing he had a chance, Alpha morphed into a Raptor. He then circled the two, climbed and hid himself in the trees and waited patiently.

Meanwhile, the teenagers didn't know what was going on and that the King was right above them. Then one of the Iguanodons stabbed his opponent with his sharp thumb spike, cutting out his windpipe and causing him to lose lots of blood. This was what Alpha was waiting for, but what he didn't realize was that he was not the only one preying on the two teenagers. As he positioned himself to pounce, he heard a loud, deep roar. A pack of large Albertosauruses, a species that was a distant relative of the T-Rex, had also been watching and now they were closing in on the same meal. Alpha knew if he faced all five of them, he would be injured, or worst. But he had no choice and took the risk.

"HAAAAAHR!!!" Alpha screeched as he leaped out of the trees and landed on the dead Iguanodon. He stood face to face with the leader of the pack and noticed the he had an arm missing due to a previous battle between them. It was Dragonfly and he was Alpha's common enemy who had tried to steal his crown.

"Greetings Alpha," said Dragonfly.

"That's Your Highness to you, Dragonfly," Alpha corrected with a snarl.

"Right." Dragonfly responded, "because you defeated me and yet, you still have your crown." "I'm sure you're aware that we are still not finished yet."

"Yes I am." Alpha said.

"Well listen, I don't feel like dealing with you today, so if you don't mind, get off of my meal!" Dragonfly commanded.

"I, The King have seen it first, so I think I will have my fair share," Alpha replied.

"Alpha, I am not a coward like everybody else on this island, OK!"

"I can see that Dragonfly," Alpha said. "But I'll ask nicely; will you surrender the food to me?"

"What, if I say no? Are you going to kill me? Dragonfly asked.

"Not *you*," Alpha said slyly.

Suddenly, he pounced on one of Dragonfly's pack members and used the killing claw on his right foot to slice off his throat. The member let out a devastating cry, clasped to the ground, and died.

"Get him!" Dragonfly commanded. Alpha ran for his life as the other Albertosauruses chased him. Once Alpha was gone, the pack went back to the feeding area and started feasting on the Iguanodon while Dragonfly knelt down next to his dead partner. His eyes suddenly turned red and his thoughts turned to . . . revenge!!!

CHAPTER 3

SHEILA

A few days had gone by and Alpha still had not eaten. Inside his den, he drew carvings of his unsuccessful hunt and his encounter with Dragonfly. As Alpha completed his carvings, he heard someone outside and went to the opening to see who was intruding. It was a female Morpher in Cheetah form, drinking out of the pond in front of his gorge.

In Lion form, Alpha stalked her silently. Reaching ground level, he began to circle her. She was so engrossed in her drinking, he went unnoticed. He rushed into the water, morphed into a large Crocodile and dove deep underwater, swimming towards her. Once he was right beneath her, he popped out of the water. "HHHHHSSSHH!!!" He hissed at her, trying to scare her off. The girl was very frightened and turned human, but didn't run away. She looked as if she was homeless-raggedy, dark hair, bruises on her body, and the only clothing she had on, were ripped animal fur skins that covered her chest and lower body.

"Who are you and what are you doing in my territory?!" he asked with a snarl as he morphed into human form also.

"I'm sorry, I-I-I was lost and thirsty," she stuttered.

"Well, finish your drink and go," Alpha said.

"But, I have nowhere to go," she reported miserably.

"Where is your family?" he asked.

"Dead!" she responded hastily. "They're all dead," she said with a weep. Everything she said so far touched Alpha because his family was also dead. "Please try to understand; I have no home," she continued. Alpha was thinking whether or not he should let her stay.

"I'm sorry to hear all of this, but usually I don't allow any strangers to stay in my gorge," Alpha explained. "What is your name?"

"My name is Sheila," she answered, still crying.

"Come Sheila." Alpha commanded. "I shall escort you to your den." He finally thought of letting her stay.

"*My* den?" She asked in surprised.

"Would you rather sleep outside in the woods?" he said, sarcastically.

"No!"

"Then follow me."

He gave her a quick tour around the gorge.

"I-I-I-I-hope you like it here," he said nervously.

Sheila had finally stopped crying, but she looked down in sorrow as she truly missed her family.

"Well, here's your den," Alpha presented. The den was empty, but it had a bed made out of rock. "Now remember this; you can go to every den on this gorge except mine," he explained.

"Why?" she asked.

"Because it's off limits!" Alpha answered quickly.

Night had fallen and the island was filled with animal calls. Alpha quickly checked the gorge to see if any creature was trespassing. Once the gorge was clear, he checked on Sheila. She was already fast asleep in wolf form, so the King headed to his den and retired for the night.

But somewhere in the bushes, two Morphers were watching Alpha and Sheila's every move. "The plan is in motion, my leader; the King has accepted her in," a boy in Hyena form whispered.

"Excellent," another Morph in Tiger form said. "Now, when the time comes, we will begin our assault," he continued with an evil grin.

Morning had at last risen which brought down a mist. The creatures were out grazing and the youngsters were out playing. Meanwhile, at the gorge, Sheila had just woken up and walked out of her den. She stretched out her front and back limbs and morphed into human form. She looked for Alpha to say good morning. Sheila knew she'd find him in his den, but remembered being told not to go to the King's cave. She called out for him but there was no response. So she took a little peek inside. Alpha was not in his den.

Sheila used her sniffing ability to try and sniff him out, but he hadn't left his scent behind. She was getting worried about this, but suddenly, her curiosity kicked in and she tip-toed inside. As Sheila walked in, she saw the carvings that Alpha drew, especially about his family's death.

Then, she saw a flash of gold light shining out of a wooded case. She eagerly removed the case and there lay a majestic Golden Bow and three Arrows. It looked so powerful Sheila couldn't resist thinking of touching it. Before she could lay a finger on it, she saw a shadow on the wall and a reflection of a Lion on the bow. Startled, she turned around. IT WAS ALPHA!!

The King had returned from another unsuccessful hunt. When he spotted her next to the bow and arrows, he leaped over, forcing Sheila away from them. He then carefully, but swiftly covered back the weapons with the wooded case. The reason he was so protective was that in his dreams, his mother said that his father had given up the weapons for him. She advised him to use them wisely while in his hands and let no one else touch them.

"What were you doing?!" he asked furiously.

"Nothing," she lied. "I-I was looking for . . .

"I told you not to come into my den! Do you realize what you could have broken?!" He scraped the walls and scratched off some of his drawings to scare her

"I'm really sorry," she cried, shaking in terror.

"Get Out!!!" he roared in rage. "GEEET OOUT NOOOOOOOOOWWWWW!!!"

Sheila ran out of there for dear life! Ten minutes had passed and Alpha finally cooled down. His feelings changed from anger to sorrow. He regretted what he said to Sheila. He placed his hand over his face and deeply sighed.

Sheila ran off to the other side of the gorge and into the woods. But she had not noticed that she ran into the wrong side known as Dinosaur Territory!!!

Chapter 4

ALPHA TO THE RESCUE!

Dinosaur Territory was home to the carnivorous dinosaurs on the island that would kill and eat any trespassers, and it was home to the leader of all the dinosaurs: Dragonfly. Sheila had never known this because she had never been there before. She kept running and running and suddenly came to a halt . . . She was surrounded by thick mist and a GIANT cornfield!

While struggling to catch her breath, she heard some rattling noises. She morphed into a Gray Wolf and ran deeper into the Heart of the territory. The noises chased her and then suddenly trapped her in thick bamboo. Sheila was terrified, but nervously positioned herself in defense mode. Suddenly, "AAAAAAL!!" "AAAAAAL!!" "AAAL!!" Ten pack members of

Raptors jumped out of the corn and surrounded Sheila, using vocalization to coordinate their attacks. Sheila tried to threaten them by snapping her jaws, but the Raptors didn't buy it. While Sheila morphed back to Human form, a Raptor tried to bite her ankle, but she was quick to react. She grew Leopard claws and started swinging her paws at the Raptors.

"Get AWAY!! HEEELP!!" She called. "AAAAHH!!" She screamed as a Raptor leaped at her, knocking and holding her down, only for another Raptor to close in.

But as the creature leaped, a vicious roar exploded in the air. The whole pack stopped in their tracks as they spotted Alpha in Bear form, sprinting towards them. He quickly tackled the leaping Raptor in midair and into the hard bamboo, shattering its hollowed bones. He tried to grab the second one, but it escaped and regrouped with the others.

Sheila froze in shock as Alpha bravely stood over her preparing for a ten on one fight. He swiftly charged at them, attacking the Raptors and trying to lead them away from Sheila. The plan had worked, but unfortunately, the creatures circled him and started using a technique "Slash and Dash."

Each of the dinosaurs jumped on the King and used their claws and teeth to slice him and then run away. Once they'd noticed that Alpha was getting dizzy and confused, they ALL piled up on him. Alpha knew he had to fight back and, with all of his might, he managed to knock them off onto the bamboo, killing four members. The Raptors then realized that if they continued to fight, they would lose more members of the pack. So the carnivores wisely retreated back to the cornfields.

Alpha triumphed in victory, but was really in bad condition from exhaustion and losing too much blood. He looked back to check on Sheila still frozen in shock. He then turned back and tried to limp home, but was very dizzy and passed out. Finally, Sheila came out of it and saw Alpha lying on the ground, barely conscious. She wanted to call out for help, but knew it would bring the attention of the Raptors and they would finish them off. So Sheila morphed into a Horse and carried him back to his lair.

CHAPTER 5

A FEELING NEVER EXPERIENCED

Sheila laid Alpha by his pond to rinse his wounds. She took a big wet leaf and gently touched his injuries. "OOOOOAAAARRRRHH!!" He howled as he woke up in pain. "That HURTS!!" he said.

"If you'd keep still, you wouldn't be in this much pain!" she responded.

"If you hadn't scurried away into Dinosaur Territory, we wouldn't have to go through all this."

"If you had not frightened me to death, I wouldn't have scurried away!"

At first Alpha didn't comment because he was furious at the time. But then he thought—

"Well, maybe you shouldn't have gone to my den and attempted to touch my golden bow and arrows, hmmm."

"Well as King, you need to control that anger of yours." She suggested.

That time, Alpha really couldn't think of anything to say, and he kept quiet. The King just looked off in defeat.

"Now hold still, this will hurt just a little bit," Sheila said in a calm voice. Once she covered his cuts with the leaf, it gave a little sting, but Alpha didn't mind it. "By the way, thanks for saving me back there."

"You're welcome," he replied surprisingly. Normally, no one on the island would say "thank you" to him, even if he did anything nice for them.

"But why?" Sheila asked.

Alpha reasoned the fact that both of their families were dead. He explained how he missed his family and especially his mother.

"Can you tell me about her?" she asked.

"Well, she was the most beautiful Morpher I had ever known. When she morphed into a wolf, she was as white as snow and had that warm voice that kept me safe and relaxed. In my dreams, she tells me everything that's going on and everything that is going to happen on this island, which led me to be prepared for anything. See Sheila, I have no one but myself."

"You have me," she reassured him. Alpha looked at her in total shock.

"What do you mean?"

She told him that she would be delighted to live with him so both wouldn't have to be alone throughout their lives. Alpha was shocked to hear this after the way he scared her half to death.

"You can do all the opposite if you would just be with someone. Trust me. I lived happy while I was with my sister, but ever since I left her alone, I changed."

"I thought your family was dead," Alpha replied.

"It's just us who survived." Sheila explained.

Alpha looked at her sadly. He knew that everything she said was true, but usually he wouldn't allow anyone to live with him.

"Are you sure?" he asked. "Because we probably won't be able to see each other until night. I mean—I have to go hunting, fight off rivals, and mark the territory, all of those things." Alpha explained.

"It's okay, I won't mind. I'll just keep a lookout for the gorge."

"It's going to be dangerous," Alpha said.

"Nothing's dangerous while I'm with you," Sheila said with confidence making Alpha chuckle.

"Thank you."

"You're welcome," Sheila replied with a smile. "Here, give me your arm. I want to try something," she said as she leaned over his arm and let a tear fall out of one eye. Once the tear landed on the wounds on his arm, they magically disappeared with no pain. Alpha looked surprised.

"The healing power of the Firebird Phoenix!" Alpha exclaimed. A Phoenix is a bird that can catch itself on fire and burn completely, but it can rebirth itself from hatchling, to adulthood.

"I got that gift from my mother," Sheila clarified.

"Wow! It must have taken a lot of practice to perfect it."

"All my life actually. But I want to try something else. This time I want you to lean back and relax," she said in a calm voice. "I want to look inside your memories."

"No, I don't think you should do that!" Alpha responded frightfully.

"Usually, I don't share my memories with anyone."

"Trust me; I know what I am doing." I just want to see your memories. Please?" she pleaded. After seeing her please puppy eyes glaring at him, he finally decided to let her look inside his memories.

"Ok."

"Just relax, and this might tickle a bit."

"Have you ever done this before?" he asked nervously.

"No!"

Alpha looked in shock and awe at her. Then, he closed his eyes and hoped for the best. Sheila hesitated at first because if she messed this up, she could kill the King. But she started to build confidence and began the process by touching his head with her first three fingers. Once she could see his memories, all she saw was his family's death. She thought that this was worst than her own family's death. When she finally stopped the process, she was filled with relief. Even though Alpha opened his eyes with a bad headache, he was more relieved than Sheila.

"Is that why?" Sheila asked.

"Yes, I would rather keep them to myself than share it with others.

"Well, your memories are safe with me," said Sheila. Alpha chuckled.

"So, did you get that from your mom too?" he asked.

"No actually, I got interested in looking through others' memories, so I trained myself," Sheila explained.

"Not bad for a beginner," Alpha said

"Thanks." Sheila replied

Two days had gone by, and the two actually turned out to be having a great time with each other. From complete strangers, to enjoying roommates, Alpha had finally found someone to be with.

One night, the bright stars and full moon shined down on Morph Island. Alpha and Sheila stayed up and watched the stars as they figured out images the stars were making.

"Oh look!" Sheila pointed out. "That looks like a baby Cheetah playing with a Butterfly. See the spots and that cute little nose."

"Yeah! Hey look!" he pointed out. "Those two look like a Lion and a Tiger fighting for the Kingdom." He laughed. "I've never done this before in my entire life."

"Really? My sister and I used to do this all the time," she chuckled. "Well, that was before I left."

Alpha assumed that she had fun hanging out with her sister, but what caused her to run away? He was also curious as to how her family died. If she knew how his family died, then why not know how hers died. She told him how her family was jealous of his because they had the Kingdom, and both became bitter rivals.

"While my family was planning for war, yours gave a surprise attack." She said. "They even killed my parents who were trying to protect my sister and me. Everyone was murdered!"

"I'm sorry," Alpha apologized, as he really felt dreadful for her. "So, why did you leave your sister?"

She told him how her sister fell in love with a Morpher who intruded their territory, and they formed a pack of Wild Dogs. She also mentioned how they would abuse them whenever she didn't make a successful hunt or if she didn't follow commands. And she was always used.

"That's cruel!" Alpha replied. "Don't worry; you'll never be abused while I'm around. I give you my word."

Sheila glared her crystal eyes at him as if she was falling for him. Next thing they knew, they were leaning their heads over as if they were about to kiss. But Alpha was first to come out of it and refused.

"We should get some sleep."

As Sheila followed Alpha up the Gorge, a female Morpher in Gray Wolf form was watching her from the bushes.

"Ok Sheila, now!" she whispered. She watched excitedly. "HUUUHH? What are you waiting for Sheila? Lead him this way!"

She watched as they went inside the den and angrily ran away and told the male Morpher, who was still in Tiger form, what happened. The tiger suddenly roared in anger causing the birds and monkeys to screech and flee through the trees.

"You're sure she didn't lead him out of the territory?" he asked.

"Yes, I saw her with my own two eyes."

"Well Sheila will not disobey us this time! And I'll make sure of it. We'll just do it the right way in the morning. Go and take three members," he ordered as they walked off into the night.

CHAPTER 6

TRAPPED

As the sun rose, it shone down on the morning mist, a beautiful sign of morning as the creatures of the island became active.

Back in the King's den where he had let Sheila sleep, he woke up and decided to leave her to slumber and bring her food. He left the den and trailed off into the woods. He only walked a few yards and spotted a small herd of Thompsons Gazelle. He decided to go for the male gazelle. Alpha knew this wasn't going to be an easy meal to catch. However, it would require the same stamina that he used when catching deer.

He morphed into Cheetah form and tried to get closer to the gazelle. When he was close enough, he waited for the meal to move towards him, and before long it did. Alpha then dipped out of the bushes. The

Gazelle turned and ran for his life along with the other gazelles. Running 70 mph in three seconds, the King was on the verge of finally catching a meal. But this buck had its own technique besides running at the same speed. It started running side to side. Alpha was getting confused and didn't know where the buck was going. But he caught up and went wherever the buck was going. Using his tail for balance, Alpha duplicated all the sharp turns his meal was taking. Suddenly, the buck tried to make a really sharp U-turn, but it tripped and slid across the grass of the plains.

Alpha seized the opportunity, leapt on the fallen Gazelle and bit down on its throat. This cut off its windpipe, causing death in a quick, yet agonizing five minutes.

Alpha carried the lifeless 150 pound buck back to the gorge. He returned to his territory but didn't see Sheila outside waiting for him.

"Sheila!" he called. "Sheila wake up!" he said growing wings and flying to the den. "Rise 'n shine! I brought some breakfast with me—a Thompsons Gazelle!" He searched for her in the den, but she wasn't there. He looked outside to see if she was in the water, or somewhere on the gorge, still not finding her. He then tried sniffing out her scent and to his delight, she had left one. But there were other scents. "Oh no!" he muttered. "Intruders have taken her!"

He picked up their scents which lead him out of the territory and back into the woods. The scent lasted a mile stopping at the river stream. The other side was a short, muddy cliff that led to higher ground. Alpha decided to swim the river that was filled with Crocodiles and Hippos. Thankfully, he made it to the other side unharmed. Suddenly, his nose picked up the scent again which led him up the cliff. To his dismay, once reaching the top, he recognized the place he had sworn never to return to . . . the Badlands. But knowing that Sheila was in there somewhere gave him the strength to persist.

The scent led him to a nearby gorge which brought him to the highest peak of the little mountain where he stopped.

"Sheila?" he whispered. To his relief, he saw her standing on a rock and climbed up to where she was.

"Sheila, there you are. I've been looking for you."

"Alpha?!" she acted suspiciously surprised to see him for some reason. "What are you doing here?"

"I've come to bring you back home"

"No, no you have to go back."

Alpha was more confused than ever seeing her acting this way. "You should not be here."

"What are you talking about?" Alpha asked as his confusion mounted.

"I-I can't really—I can't. Look, just go please!"

"No, I am not leaving without you!"

Suddenly, a low growl startled them. Turning around, they saw the Wild Dogs that Sheila described as Domestic Dogs, wolves, African Wild Dogs, jackals, coyotes and even hyenas come into sight from above and below. Then Alpha spotted the male tiger and the female Gray Wolf walk out the den that was behind them. They both then realized that they were SURROUNDED!!!

"Get behind me," Alpha ordered Sheila.

"Now, now, is this any way to treat a guest; especially, if our little guest is our King. Oh, I'm sorry;

I mean the Last King!" The tiger criticized. "Welcome Alpha."

"And, may I ask, who are you?" Alpha asked.

"Oh you know who I am Alpha. You don't remember that it wasn't just you who survived the eruption as a hatchling. You see, there was another baby in his egg that came close to being smashed by a boulder. A few days later, after we hatched, he was also raised by the Meerkat family. He wanted to play with you; he only wanted to play with you! But since you were so annoyed when they told you about our family, you viciously ripped off a piece of his right ear, exiled him from the territory and ordered that he never come back!"

As he told the story, the memories made his anger return. But with an evil grin, he began to calm down.

"Well that kid, Alpha, was me!!" he finally revealed himself. "That's right. It's me, your brother, Usarian."

Alpha looked in complete shock that he even had a brother.

"No, all of my family died." said Alpha refusing to believe Usarian.

"Brother, don't you see, your dreams were lying to you. And so, I am taking what is rightfully mine; *my* home, and *my* Throne. Thanks to my lovely assistant right there," he said, pointing to Sheila. "She's the one who brought you here to finish what had been started. It's really heartbreaking when your first love betrays you like this. It's a good thing I could trust her beautiful sister, Nira because we are too connected for her to betray me. Isn't that right my flower?"

"Yes my love," she responded, showing her affection for him by rubbing her body against him.

Alpha, so devastated about what he had just heard, turned to Sheila who was looking down in shame and despair.

"Is this true?"

"Yes."

"So, all the time we had together, all the things I've done for you was all part of the plan, huh?" I knew I should've followed my instincts and left you to fend for yourself against the Raptors." He thought out loud.

"OOOOH, harsh don't you think?" Usarian interrupted.

"SILENCE!!!" Alpha demanded.

"As far as I'm concerned, you are no better than the enemies that I had to deal with all my life. Sheila, you don't deserve to be loved. I guess you just deserve to be a slave after all." Alpha said, trying not to let her know how hurt he was.

He then turned to his brother. "Now as for you Usarian, you are not taking the throne away from me that easily."

"If I may recall, two Morphers and thirteen wild dogs against one Morpher King, means that there is a great possibility that I could kill you for the throne without effort." He insulted. Suddenly, Alpha walked up to him, swung his right fist and punched him with such force, that it knocked Usarian down. Alpha tried to run away, but Usarian recovered and ordered his pack to kill him.

"NOOOO!!!" Sheila looked in horror seeing the one she still loved get brutally attacked by the dogs.

The dogs pounced on him, continuing to bite him. Alpha quickly morphed into Lion form and shook most of the dogs off.

"Stop!" Sheila demanded, running up to Usarian who was enjoying the view. "This is madness!"

"Oh I'll tell you what madness is," Usarian responded. "Madness was why I never got to be King in the first place!"

"You're a monster." Sheila shouted.

"Isn't that what all of us Morphers are? Monsters?" he asked with an evil grin. "Sorry Sheila, but life just isn't fair at all."

He then unexpectedly, back-slapped her across the face knocking her out. Her sister, Nira showed no pity or sympathy for her sister and enjoyed this. She then turned her attention to the fight. She positioned herself and leaped on the King, causing him to fall ten feet down along the gorge and hitting the ground.

"That's it! We got him now, boys!" Usarian yelled.

Then he ran down the mountain with the pack and shoved Alpha off the entry ledge into the little river stream. The pack swam after him. They all made it across except for one Jackal who was violently caught in the jaws of the Crocodile. Alpha reached land and began to run, with each move causing him great pain, but if he was to survive, had to keep going. With all of his speed and agility, he desperately tried to outrun the pack, but they seemed to always be catching up. "Circle him!" Usarian instructed. Nira and two other dogs leaped onto the branches of the trees, outran Alpha and stopped him in his tracks as they jumped down to the ground landing right in front of him. Alpha wanted to turn back and run, but his brother and the rest of the pack were catching up real swiftly.

Alpha desperately looked for an escape route. He looked to his left and he could see an animal herd in the opening through the bushes. If he could cause a stampede, he could lose the dogs and Usarian. That would put him at risk of being trampled, but it was a necessary risk and he decided to go for it.

"GRRRR," "RUFF, RUFF," "AOOOOOOOOHH!" The dogs barked and howled as the chase continued. As Alpha reached the herd, the animals got frightened and scattered. The plan was in motion; all the King had to do was to stay inside the herd.

Meanwhile, Usarian knew what was going on, so he and the dogs tried to figure out how to isolate him from the herd. Then he came up with another idea.

"Don't do anything," he instructed. "Wait until we reach the Triceratop's territory. We can finish him there. But keep the herd at bay."

Alpha stayed inside the herd, and could see the dogs running after them, but they weren't getting close. He knew that they were up to something. A few yards away, Alpha could see that the herd was headed towards the Triceratops. This was what the pack had been waiting for.

Once the Triceratops saw the panicking herd, they started to become alarmed. Now all the creatures were running for dear life, vibrating the island as the massive weight of feet and hooves rapidly stomped the ground.

"Now's our chance. Separate into two and scout him out." Usarian instructed.

The separate groups forced themselves into the herd. Then two Hyenas located Alpha. They made siren calls to alert the other members. "WOOP!!" "WOOP!!" "WOOP!!" Alpha could hear them closing in on him. The two Hyenas reached up to speeds of 50 mph.

Before Alpha could continue to outwit them, he noticed a cliff up ahead. The Morphers called the cliff the "Island's Edge." If Alpha turned back, the dogs would end him for sure. He had to find another route. He saw an open spot and took it. Thankfully, the King made it and was out of harm's way. Unfortunately for the pack, they never realized about the edge until it was too late. One dog had fallen off with some of the animals while the others avoided the plunge. Alpha couldn't bear to watch. He ran to his home, with some bite wounds. Once everything got calmed, the remaining herd ran back to their feeding grounds while Usarian, Nira and the other dogs regrouped.

"See what happened?! See what you've done?!" Nira accused Usarian. "You just *had* to pick Sheila to do the task."

"Nira relax," Usarian said calmingly.

"I should've done it! But no, you just had to choose her even after I warned how stubborn she could be."

"The reason I didn't pick you, was because I needed someone in the group who had the same past and also felt lonely and depressed like Alpha. Sheila was the perfect match." Usarian explained. "It turned out, she was too involved and failed. But there is no need to worry. Thanks to you, the King is now injured and weak, and so, at dusk, we will attack." He laughed, as he couldn't wait for tomorrow.

Meanwhile, Sheila recovered from Usarian's attack and caught up to where the chase ended. She hid in the bushes where Alpha had dodged the edge. She heard every word they said.

"I've got to warn Alpha," Sheila whispered to herself as she ran back to his gorge.

CHAPTER 7

EXILED FROM THE GORGE

When Sheila arrived at the gorge, she began frantically searching for Alpha not knowing he had not arrived yet. She had to warn him about the deadly plan his brother had for him.

As she moved about the gorge, she found a 16 foot Giant Ground Sloth searching for any tasty fruits to eat. When the Sloth picked up her scent and spotted her, the beast made a huge screech and charged at her. Sheila ran down the gorge, but tripped over a rock and fell all the way down to the terrain. When she got up and looked back, the monster was on her tail. She tried to escape into the woods from where she came, but the

Sloth began to circle, forcing her to run straight into Dinosaur Territory.

Sheila realized she was back in this environment and wanted to turn back. When she turned, the Sloth reared up on its hind legs. This made it rise to 32 feet, terrifying Sheila, because it took on the appearance of a walking oak tree. She was terrified and didn't know what to do. But, she stood her ground while being, just a few feet away from the cornfields.

Meanwhile, Alpha had just entered his territory, still limping from his wounds. He wasn't aware that Sheila was in a load of trouble until . . . "AAAAAAH!!!" He heard Sheila scream. He then realized that she was in Dinosaur Territory again where he had saved her from the flesh eating Raptors. But after what he had just been through, Alpha was thinking whether to save her or leave her for being a traitor. He finally chose to save her again and he ran off into the woods.

As soon as he was in, he noticed a giant, brown, fuzzy wall.

"That wasn't there before," he mumbled. Then suddenly, it moved! When Alpha saw a head in sight, he realized that it was the Ground Sloth.

"RRROOOOAAAARR!!!" the Sloth let out another huge cry.

"Alpha! Help!" Alpha looked to the side of the colossal beast and saw Sheila trying to defend herself.

"Hang in there Sheila!"

Then the monster turned around and spotted him. It held up its left paw that contained four claws and swung at Alpha. The King quickly dodged the attack and morphed into a Sabre-Tooth Tiger. He crouched on his belly, waiting and looking for the right moment to attack and do this quickly. Sheila tried to take advantage of the distraction and bit the Sloth's ankle. The creature screeched in pain, but kicked its foot out, knocking Sheila into a tree, which then gave Alpha the opportunity to pounce on the Sloth. He tried to use his long, serrated, knife-like front teeth to give a death blow to its throat, but the beast kept shaking, causing him to loosen his grip and fall. Once the Sloth sensed that the King had fallen back onto the ground, he then bit his ankle. "AAAAARRRRHHH!!!" Alpha cried in severe pain. Suddenly, out of nowhere, Sheila leapt onto its back and used her claw to stab its eye tearing it out of its socket.

"RRAAAOORR!!!" The Sloth howled as it slowly ran away in defeat. Sheila kicked away the exposed eye.

"Are you all right?" Sheila asked breathing heavily.

"I'm fine,"

"Aren't you going to thank me?"

"No!"

"But I just saved your life and I don't get a thank you?" she asked, beginning to get upset.

"That's right, because you don't deserve it," he said as he limped back to his home while Sheila followed. "You know Sheila," he continued. "I thought you were the one. I thought that it was real for me. But maybe my dreams were lying to me. Thanks to you, I now know who you really are. You're one of those mindless tricksters who spellbind others just to save your own skin. And of course I'm the flawless victim who got played because I am the ultimate prize."

He then sank his wounded ankle into the pond to wash it out.

"Now you listen to me," Sheila responded, really irritated from all he had said. "Everything you just said about me was a lie. I didn't trick you into falling in love with me. It was real for me too. Ever since I met you, I hoped you would accept me as your mate."

"Why? Because of what we have in common?" Alpha interrupted. He told her he was no longer bothered by the fact that both of their families were dead. He also shared that she didn't deserve to live with him.

"SSSS!! OW!" he hissed in pain as he continued to rinse his wounds.

"You need me to fix that?" Sheila asked, changing the subject as she tried to keep her feelings in.

"No."

"Fine. If you insist on limping around and getting pounded on during your fight with your twisted brother, then be my guest."

"Fight?!" Alpha asked in shock.

"Yes. Your crown and life are going to be on the line."

Alpha had no choice, but to let her heal his injury. Sheila leaned down and let a tear fall down on his bite wound. Once again when it landed, the injury disappeared. Alpha even let her heal his wounds from the fight against the dogs.

"This doesn't change anything between us, Sheila. We're done."

"What do you mean?"

"Well, if you weren't listening to me, let me just say, I never want to see you again ever!" he yelled. "So I hereby proclaim, you are exiled from the territory."

"Wait you can't exile me! You're going to need my help. You need me.

"Trust me; I've been through the worst and, I don't need your help."

"No. "You haven't!" Sheila corrected. "If you want to keep that little throne of yours, then you will let me help you."

"All I need are all of my skills and techniques.".

"But Alpha; he is your brother!" she said raising her tone. "He knows you well and there are great possibilities that he can be more lethal, and more agile than you. Trust me. I know him more than you do."

"Well I guess I should get to know my brother more in person."

"Do that and he'll kill you!"

"Thanks for all the information. Now get out!" He said as he started walking up to his gorge, but Sheila cut him off.

"Look, you don't have to do this alone Alpha," Sheila bellowed. "The truth is, you are the only one I have and I just can't watch you die out there," she said in a stressful tone.

Taking her thoughts into consideration, he began to rethink renouncing her exile.

"You know, I actually thought that deep down, you had a heart to forgive like all the other Morphers, but I guess you're not the King who'd do that." Sheila said.

"First of all, it's just five of us Morphers on this island and none of us can forgive. It's our way of surviving and, yes, you're right. "Never have I forgiven a traitor or an enemy. That's part of the reason I'm still King." Alpha said.

"I'm just really disappointed in you." Shelia replied.

"You know that sounds like something my mother would say." Alpha compared.

"Great," she said. "At least someone besides your mother can talk to you with wisdom." Alpha made a sudden frown and went off on her.

"Ok, you know what?!" Alpha yelled. "You think you could just trespass into my territory and tell me how I should live my life as King? You have no clue how much I have been through!

He once again asked her to leave his gorge.

"You know what?!" Sheila shouted temperedly. "Fine! But once I leave, I'm never coming back." She then turned and walked away.

"Good," Alpha yelled after her. "I don't need a worthless traitor to help me with my issues."

Sheila halted. Suddenly, her eyes shaded in red color. She then grew 2 inch retractable claws on her right paw and swung and made a huge impact to Alpha's face. Alpha let out a shriek, his face dripping with blood.

"Well, what I don't need is to help a stubborn, selfish, ignorant King who doesn't care for anyone but himself."

Alpha looked at her as she angrily walked away, through the bushes and into the woods. As he was clenching onto his face to stop the bleeding, he thought to himself, feeling guilty, "Was it worth it? Can I handle this battle by myself?"

Night had fallen and the animals were letting out their calls. On the top of the Gorge was Alpha, who was also joining the crowd. But he was making those calls to let the whole island know that he was going to be putting his kingdom on the line, for he would soon be in a vicious clash. He trumpeted, roared, howled, and hissed. By using those sounds, everyone knew he was ready.

As Alpha was getting ready to go to sleep, he was still thinking of what Sheila said and how she felt. He touched his healing wounds on his face which were caused by calling Sheila a traitor. He tried so hard to fight off those thoughts, but his guilt just kept rising. He even spotted his mother's ghost from behind, shaking her head in shame and then suddenly disappeared. He then heard her speak. She told him she was disappointed and that, there would be consequences. Once the voices stopped, Alpha looked up at his drawings next to the cave entrance. Turning away, he suddenly, saw a picture that he never carved, and realized it was illustrated by Sheila. It showed them lying on the grasslands covered in flowers. Then he noticed the words at the bottom of the carving; words that struck his heart. It spelled out, "TOGETHER FOREVER." Because of that, Alpha's guilt increased rapidly and caused him to shed tears. He really wanted her to come back, but remembered that he had already vowed that she could never come back.

Over in the badlands, Usarian, Nira, and the dogs were also getting prepared for the upcoming battle. Unexpectedly, they spotted Sheila returning.

"Hey, look who had the guts to show up," a Jackal said with a chuckle. Nira came out, not too delighted to see her sister.

"What are you doing back here?" she asked with a snarl. "You don't belong here! You belong with that cowardly King that we are going to demolish!"

"Peace, my flower," Usarian ordered as he listened to the threats. "I'm sure there's an explanation for this." Everyone gazed at her, anxiously waiting to hear why she had returned with a determined look.

"Look, I know I've messed up everything, even the trap," Sheila answered. "But I want to make it up to you all. I want to join you in the battle."

First, everyone was confused for they thought that she was just kidding. But she gave details of everything Alpha did to her and she wanted revenge. The dogs and Nira couldn't decide whether to just ban her, or accept her in the pack. Nira stated that she'd rather have her sister be an outcast than be in their pack.

All of the bickering gave Usarian an idea to do more than fight his brother.

"Enough!" Usarian shouted. "I have an idea."

He explained that they'd use Sheila in the fight for a distraction. He knew it would break Alpha's heart to see Sheila joining the enemy's side. The dogs agreed and howled as they welcomed her back into the pack.

"HAHAHA!!" Usarian laughed. "Can you all even imagine the things that we will achieve?" he asked the rest of the pack. "Can you feel the success? Can you taste the accomplishments as we celebrate our victory?! HAHAHAHAHAHA!!" He laughed again. Then he escorted Sheila into their den.

"Alpha won't do anything to you if he had the chance because you're his first heart and pride. Now thanks to you, we have the advantage and the Kingdom will be in our hands," he said. "And if you stay in our pack, I promise you, you can start a whole new life and family and you'll be a slave no more," he whispered in her ear. "You can be free and have all the things that you desire. I can grant those things. So if I were you, I wouldn't disappoint me again." Sheila was so happy to hear that, she couldn't stop laughing to herself as she thought about what she'd done if the pack had taken over as rulers. Then she couldn't wait for the fight.

Behind the cave entrance, Nira looked at her sister, already predicting that there was likely going to be a screw up during the battle. And Sheila was going to be the perpetrator once again.

CHAPTER 8

CLASH OF THE RIVALRIES

Morning had finally arrived, bringing clouds to the sky. But Usarian, in Tiger form, Nira and Sheila in Gray Wolf form, and the rest of the pack were already on their way to the Gorge. They only had one thing on their minds, and that was to decimate and kill the King and rule the Island before the volcano erupted for the last time. All the creatures in the woods retreated out of their way as the pack walked in full force. The monkeys and the birds chirped and made screaming noises as they were alerting all the creatures that the pack was on the move.

After going through all the noises of the woods, the pack finally arrived at the Gorge. Once they looked up, they spotted Alpha standing on a ledge with paint markings all over his body. Alpha then grew Gryphon wings, leaped off the Gorge and landed softly on the ground. But once he landed, what he saw amazed and broke his heart at the same time. He gazed at Sheila standing next to Usarian.

"Surprised?" Usarian asked. "I thought you would be." And what's more astonishing is, she wanted to join us. But I'll offer you a choice. Give up your throne, and I'll hand over her to you or, you will suffer the most brutal attack that the pack and I have ever administered. So there is still time for you to surrender the throne."

"Or fight for it," Alpha responded.

"HHHUUHHHH!" Usarian huffed. "Must it all end in violence? Listen brother, we don't have to do this. All I want is for you to end your reign and give the Kingdom to me before this home goes down to the bottom of the ocean."

"Sorry brother," Alpha said. "Unfortunately, for you, I am never going to surrender my throne to anyone. I'll make sure of it."

"So be it," Usarian replied. "This will start as a single combat fight. You win, then you'll have to face me, my flower Nira, the pack and Sheila," he explained. For a minute, Alpha turned and looked at Sheila with a nearly depressed look on his face. Then he turned back to his brother.

"Agreed," Alpha said as he morphed into Lion form.

As Usarian was still a Tiger, they sized up each other. Then Nira, Sheila and the pack formed a wide circle around the two brothers.

"Say good bye to your Kingdom, brother," Usarian taunted with an evil grin. Alpha began pouncing on him, but Usarian shook him off rapidly. Alpha viciously swung at him with his paw. The impact had built up Usarian's anger. He furiously jumped on Alpha. Alpha tried to counter his brother's attacks, but Usarian knew how to come back.

The dogs meanwhile howled, barked, and made whooping noises to cheer on their leader. Suddenly, Usarian pounced on top of Alpha and tried to go for the neck bite, but Alpha was quick enough to flip him over. They then both morphed into Human form. Alpha charged at him, but Usarian also charged and tackled him through the circle. He then bit his brother's left arm. Alpha screeched in agony and desperately tried to use his other arm to punch Usarian in the gut, but he missed.

"You know Alpha," he said while he watched his brother cling onto his injured arm. "I really hate to tell you this, but as your brother, frankly, I'm a little disappointed."

Alpha then tried to get back up.

"Stay down!" Usarian commanded.

Then all of a sudden, the King snapped!! He morphed into an 11 foot Short-Faced Bear and back-slapped his brother with such force, it caused Usarian to fly 4 feet into the air. Then he started going after the dogs. He swung at an African Wild Dog, grabbed one of the Hyenas in his jaws and threw him to the Gorge. The other Hyena and a Jackal bit his ankle and flanks and every dog, including Nira got involved. Alpha used his power to fight them off. He pounded every dog in the pack, including Nira. He was about to pound the last member, but the last one was Sheila. Alpha paused from pounding her. He never realized she was really distracting him on purpose. The plan went perfectly as Usarian grew a Carnotaur tail and smacked Alpha from behind. The impact sent Alpha flying and he crashed into the gorge.

Sheila actually enjoyed the scene at first, but she then had thoughts of her and Alpha together and how they could've lived a happy life. But she then erased that thought and remembered what Usarian told her about becoming free from being a slave if she'd done what he told her to do to the King.

"Come on Sheila," Usarian interrupted. "Let's make this Kingdom ours once and for all."

Unfortunately, the King was not in good condition. He was back in Human form as he clutched onto his left side. When he looked up, he saw Usarian and Sheila move stealthily towards him. He tried to get up, but his left shoulder kept giving in. As the two bared their teeth and made low growls, Sheila's thought of freedom was still on her mind. Looking at the King, who was defenseless, the thought of the two of them together came up again. Only this time, she and Alpha ruled the Kingdom together. Alpha told her that if Usarian won the throne, he would still make her a slave and that it was going to be worse than it was before. Sheila couldn't take the thoughts anymore. Suddenly, as Usarian was about to attack, Sheila circled him and stopped him in his tracks with a snarl. Usarian looked puzzled and irritated.

"What are you doing?!"

"Something that I should've been doing," Sheila answered with confidence. "Sorry Usarian, but I reject that little offer of yours. You wicked fraud; I know you were lying to me about my freedom," she continued. "And now, I am dropping out of your pack of mutts and going to help the King decimate each and every one of you!" Usarian looked at her, still irritated. Then he saw Nira and the rest of the dogs walk up next to him.

"Ok," he responded. "If this is how it's going to be, fine. But I will not have you fail us this time, so, I intend to take you out first."

He then circled her, trying to separate her from Alpha who was still down and stunned from the impact. But Sheila stood her ground. She morphed into a beautiful red and white Horse. Usarian tried swiping his claws and nipping his teeth at her to back her away from the area. Sheila kept dodging his attacks and stood on her hind legs. Out of nowhere, Nira was crouching above Sheila on the Gorge. Once her target was positioned, she pounced and landed on Sheila's back. This caused Sheila to panic and sprint away from the King. This gave Usarian a chance to finish his weakened brother off while the other members decided to help Nira. Sheila furiously kicked her sister off of her causing her to land on Usarian. She then charged at him.

She led him away as she stood on her hind legs again and kicked with her front limbs. She then morphed into a kangaroo, stood on her muscled tail and viciously kicked his jaw. Thinking that he was now down and stunned, she morphed into the mystical unicorn and galloped to him with the 4 inch horn, ready to kill. But Usarian unexpectedly recovered from the kick, heard Sheila coming and quickly grabbed and squeezed her throat.

"AAAAAAHH!!" Sheila screamed as she became human.

"I only slapped you because I didn't feel like killing you and so that you'd stay out my way," Usarian explained. "But you just keep on pissing me off. So how about this time, I kill you?"

"Usarian!!!"

He looked over and what he saw astonished him. It was Alpha himself, ready to fight. Usarian threw Sheila down in anger.

The two brothers then charged at each other. They leaped in the air at the same time, but Alpha speared Usarian back 3 feet down to the ground. Nira then tried to get involved in it by creeping up on the King and positioned herself to pounce. But Sheila was quick to react and leaped on her and bit her on the shoulder. Now the sisters clashed. Then the dogs went to help Nira and Usarian. The two bitter rival brothers had sliced and bit each other until Usarian knocked his brother down on his spine. Then painfully, he shoved 3 inch claws into Alpha's shoulders. Alpha cried out in pain.

"This Kingdom is mine!" Usarian blurted.

Then all of the sudden, "RROOOOOAAAARRR!!!" a roar echoed out into the air. And it came out of Dinosaur Territory. Everyone stopped and they looked around curiously. Usarian took his claws out of Alpha and tried to get a closer look through the woods. Then, they heard heavy footsteps which caused the ground to tremble, coming closer and closer.

Suddenly, a 34 foot tall dinosaur came out. It was the Albertosaurus, Dragonfly, along with fifteen other dinosaurs such as Raptors, Oviraptors, Trodons, and Pachycephlosauruses. The thirteen dogs and Nira stood alongside Usarian, forming a blockade. The leaders, Usarian and Dragonfly went face to face with each other as neither of them were happy about what was going on.

"Who are you and why are you interfering with my fight for my throne?" Usarian asked.

"I am Dragonfly, the King's nemesis and I believe that it is *my* fight for my throne." "Well it looks to me that you're too late, Dragonfly," Usarian said.

"So, you must be Usarian, Alpha's brother. I can tell because just like your brother, you're stubborn."

Meanwhile, Sheila took advantage of the distraction and helped Alpha up the gorge. They then hid behind a boulder where they could see the commotion.

Are you all right?" she asked.

"Yeah," Alpha answered in pain.

"Listen Alpha, I am so sorry for being on your brother's side." She apologized.

"No, no it's not your fault." Alpha revised. "I'm sorry for calling you a traitor. I was aware that you were going to join his side for what I did and I forgive you."

Sheila then hugged him and shed a tear as feeling guilty for turning her back on him. "The truth is; I really missed you last night." He admitted.

"But I was only gone for the night," she said.

"I guess I'm so used to having you sleep with me every night that I can't be separated from you, even if it is just for one night," Alpha said, with his feelings becoming stronger for her.

Back on the ground, Dragonfly was trying to convince Usarian to join forces with each other against Alpha and the island together, but, Usarian declined the offer and shouted for his pack to attack. Now it's was Wild Dogs vs. Dinosaurs.

But as they started ripping each other apart, the island suddenly started to shake. The animals halted their browsing and panicked, except the fighting Morphers. This made Usarian remember his unfinished business with his brother. Then, as volcanic ash fell from the sky, he realized that time was almost at its limit. Alpha looked up at his den.

"Stay here," he ordered Sheila.

"Where are you going?"

"I have to get something that may be my only weapon to defeat Usarian and Dragonfly," He then looked back to the ground. "Ah!" he grunted. "It looks like the fight is going to be on this Gorge. Ok listen to me." He began to whisper. "At the highest peak of this mountain, there's a small hole that should take you to the other side of the Gorge, out of harm's way. I want you to find it go through it."

"Wait, Alpha."

She came up to him and gave him a kiss on the cheek.

"Be careful."

Alpha nodded and ran away while Sheila went on her search for her escape hole. As the ashes kept falling, the island got darker. But the Morphers had strong night vision and were able to continue their search. While Alpha climbed up to his den, Usarian was also scouting on the Gorge.

"Don't let Dragonfly or his dino freaks place a claw on Alpha," he yelled to his pack. "He's mine!"

Alpha had finally reached inside his den. He was going after his dad's Golden Bow and Arrows.

Meanwhile, his brother was still looking for him. But the person he found was not Alpha; it was Sheila. She was still seeking for the hole through the ashes. He silently stalked her from behind still wanting to kill her for what she had done earlier. He accidentally stepped on rock, which fell down the gorge startling Sheila who looked back to see what caused the rock to fall. With her night vision, she could see Usarian running towards her and quickly climbed up the gorge to escape.

Back in the King's den, Alpha put the bow over his chest and placed the arrows in the arrow case which also hung from his chest. As he headed for the open, he heard Sheila scream. When he looked outside, he saw Sheila climbing really fast, but when he looked behind her, the sight sent chills down his spine. Usarian was pursuing her. Sheila took cover in the cave that she first slept in. Alpha rushed over while still setting up his weapon. He stopped to take aim. He fired. The arrow dashed and sliced a piece of Usarian's arm to the rocks. And then, the arrow made a big golden explosion which caused some big rocks to fall. The boulders caused Sheila to be caved in. The arrow was designed to make explosions which kill by blowing a foe completely to bits. Unluckily, Alpha missed.

Once Usarian spotted Alpha looking at him so angrily, he ran. Alpha morphed into Lion form, dropped his weapon and pursued him. Usarian led his brother to the top of the gorge, which was 40 feet high. The winds picked up, making the ash flakes scatter everywhere.

"Alpha I'm sure you know where we are," Usarian yelled. "This is where you and I used to play-fight all the time."

"Really?" Alpha asked. "Well I guess there won't be any play-fighting now, huh?"

"HmHm!!" "I knew you were going to say that," Usarian said. "Tell me Alpha. Are you willing to kill your own brother?"

"No Usarian. You see, I'm not like you and I'll never be anything like you. I won't kill you, but I'll make you rot on this island as it burns to the ocean and you'll go down with it." Alpha said.

"But you are just like me Alpha. You just won't admit it." Usarian said with an evil, grinning smile. Suddenly, he morphed into a dragon and flapped his wings outward. This caused the ash flakes to cluster into Alpha's eyes.

"AAAAAHH!!!" Alpha cried, trying to wipe the ashes out of his eyes. Then Usarian pounced on him and bit him on his back. Alpha rolled over trying to get out of his grip, but Usarian held on. He was on Alpha, about to bite him again, but he kicked him off and jumped him. He tried to swing with his right paw, but his brother caught him with his teeth, causing Alpha to roar in pain. He then swung his other paw with force and connected to his brother's face. Usarian swung back with a Dragon tail causing Alpha to fall on his back. Usarian then pounced. Alpha then tried to flip him over, but Usarian held on, causing both of them to fall halfway down the Gorge.

Alpha caught onto a ledge. He tried to pull himself on top, but suddenly, Dragonfly, now in Raptor form, bit his right limb with curved, serrated teeth.

"OOOOOWW!!!" Alpha cried.

Next thing he saw above him was his brother, positioned to pounce. Alpha quickly grew a whip tail and lashed at him. The blow stunned Dragonfly and caused him to release his bite. Alpha forced himself on top of the ledge, but Usarian had already pounced. Alpha tried to pounce, but his injured leg gave way. Usarian landed on him, but Alpha rolled backwards, causing all of them to fall down the Gorge. This time, they fell all the way down to the ground, along with Dragonfly.

CHAPTER 9

THE ERUPTION ESCAPE

The shock of seeing all three rivals land onto the terrain, caused everyone to stop fighting. The Wild Dogs and the Dinosaurs gazed over at their leaders and Alpha as the three recovered from their plunge. They circled each other stealthily and were filled with rage. Then . . .

"AAAAAHHRRRRGGH!!!" Dragonfly screeched.
"HHHRRRROOOAAAARRR!!" Usarian roared.
"RRRROOOOAAAR!!!" Alpha roared.

They were about to finish each other off. Just as they were about to make their final blows, the island started to shake again. But this time, it shook more rapidly than the last quake. The Morphers then began to fret. They were desperately trying to keep their balances. Then, the quake suddenly stopped. What looked like a bad situation suddenly turned catastrophic. Through the thick darkness of the ashes, every Morpher could see lava shooting out of the volcano. They slowly began to realize that the volcano had erupted! All living life forms on the island watched in horror at the scene.

Fireballs of every size rained down on the battleground beginning to cover the whole island. The Dogs and the Dinosaurs panicked and ran including Nira. Meanwhile, determined to finish the fight, Usarian grew a clubbed tail and swung it at Dragonfly and connected. Alpha tried to take advantage and charged at him, but Usarian was too quick to react and instead grabbed him by the throat, swung him 180 degrees and slammed him to the ground with power.

"No more games brother. Say hi to mother for me!" Usarian mocked, as he put a killing claw on his finger to finish him off.

Suddenly, a fireball landed just 2 feet away from the brothers. Usarian realized that he had a spark of fire on his shoulder. He tried to put it out which gave Alpha the chance to punch and flip him over. The King watched as Usarian got dropped by a colossal fireball and eventually disappeared through the ash.

Alpha was about to depart off the island when he realized that Sheila was still trapped in the cave. He hastily morphed into a cheetah and sprinted to the Gorge. He climbed up the rocks and ledges until he reached the cave. He used power and strength of an Elephant to remove the boulders that were blocking the cave entrance. Once he removed the rocks, he could see that Sheila was still inside, but was lying down unconscious.

"Sheila!" he called trying to wake her up.

He knew that it was only a matter of time to get her and him off the island. So, he placed her on his back and went back outside. Next thing he realized, there were giant boulders rolling down the Gorge. The King thankfully avoided the rocks as he slid and ran down to the ground and made it into the woods, which were already engulfed in flames. Alpha frantically avoided ignited trees. He then spotted creatures running in the woods as they were being burned alive. He felt really terrible for them, especially for the infants because they didn't stand a chance. No one and nothing could save them now. The two had reached Usarian's territory which was consumed by flames. A couple yards ahead, Alpha could see the Island's Edge. Once he got close, he halted.

He looked down at the ocean and remembered that it was filled with man-eating sea creatures such as; Mega Sharks, Sea Scorpions, Mosasaursuses, Plesiosauruses, the Kraken and much more. But when Alpha looked back to check on Sheila, still unconscious, he saw a humongous, terrifying ash cloud devouring everything in its path on the island, heading straight towards him. It was moving fast.

Alpha had no choice but to turn and jump off the island. The two plunged 30 feet down and into the ocean. Once Alpha surfaced, he realized Sheila was missing, but she then came into view. Alpha swam desperately towards her. She was half awake, and confused about her whereabouts.

"I got you Sheila," Alpha said, grabbing her before she could sink again.

Suddenly, two giant tentacles from the Kraken reared 40 feet out of the water, ready to pound down on Alpha and Sheila. But just in time, a fireball crashed through one of the tentacles, breaking it in half. The monster made a loud, cold, spine-chilling shriek that could be heard on the surface and into the skies. Suddenly, three fireballs hit the second tentacle. This time, the beast made another shriek, forcing Alpha to cover his ears. The Kraken retreated his tentacles back into the water in defeat.

Just when Alpha hoped he was able to continue his swim, a tidal wave rose 66 feet in the air behind them. The King tried to out swim it, but the wave dropped and pulled Alpha and Sheila underwater.

Chapter 10

AMBI ENCOUNTERS

Once the catastrophe was over, it left a horrible sight. The island was still ignited, and lava plunged down from the island and into parts of the ocean. It was like Hell opened up and preyed on the beloved island. All the creatures on the island were dead, including the little infants. It was just as terrible as the sheol itself.

Alpha landed on the other side of the ocean. He was unconscious, but alive. A few hours had passed and he had finally awakened. It took him about ten minutes to get a footing. When he sadly looked at his surroundings, all he saw were bits of fire and heavy smoke covering the sky. Then, he noticed that Sheila was gone once again. He looked in the water, holding his breath, nothing. He then made screeching cries of the Raptor. No response. He let out another call. No answer. When he finally gave up, he had to assume that she either drowned, or was eaten by a sea monster. Either way, Alpha had to get over the fact that she was dead. He slowly began to realize he was going to live alone again. Only, this time, it would be forever. Alpha turned to see the island he was going to call "HOME." As he got ready to head out on his exploration for this unknown island, he heard low whispers calling his name.

"Alpha, Alpha." He turned back and saw a familiar face. It was Sheila! Determined to be back in Alpha's presence, she desperately crawled out of the ocean and onto the land.

"Sheila," he called as he ran to her and gave her a hug. "I thought you were dead."

"I told you I would never leave you," Sheila said.

"Alpha I am so sore, I can barely move." She complained.

"Listen to me," he instructed. "I'm going to get you out of here, all right?" he reassured her, as he morphed into a Bull Elephant and lifted her on his back with his extended trunk.

He took one last look at his fallen Kingdom. He then looked up at the sky and saw a flock of birds flying through the smoky air. Usually, when birds fly, they lead other creatures to food, water, or shelter. And so, Alpha followed them into the strange new island.

When they traveled further into the island, they found themselves in a desert, where the temperature was 140 degrees Celsius and rising. Meanwhile, Sheila just woke up from a nap. She was no longer sore. She looked around the environment and was confused.

"Where are we?" she asked.

"Well," Alpha responded. "This is actually the island I visited in my dreams. And it is so unique, not only does it contain a Desert environment, which is where we are right now, but it also has a Forest environment. Once we get to the Forest, we'll just settle in and call it home."

"Did you see any creatures on this island in your dreams?" she asked.

"No," he said. "It was like, it was deserted." "But I heard rumors saying that this island was populated with creatures."

"What is this place?"

"Ambi Island," Alpha said, "named for its two environments." Alpha looked back at Sheila. He could see she wasn't feeling too well. "Are you all right?"

"OOOOHHH!!" Sheila moaned. "I'm so thirsty." Alpha then came to a halt.

"Here," he said. "In my dreams, my mom taught me that once you had drunken water, you can keep it in for as long as you live without it affecting your digestive process. Well, I kept a stomach full of water in me for all my life."

He then started digging a hole in the sand. Then, he put his trunk in his mouth and regurgitated a half gallon of water into his trunk and poured it into the hole.

"Once you regurgitate the water, it comes out fresh with no bacteria. So now, I provide this to you." Sheila climbed off of Alpha's back.

"Thank you," she said with relief and began drinking the water. When she finally finished drinking, she climbed back on Alpha's back and they kept moving for another mile. Alpha started to sniff the air with his extensive truck.

"Hey wait a minute," he said as he stopped in his footsteps.

"What is it?"

"I can smell greens and fresh water," he responded. "Can you smell that?" he asked excitedly. Sheila sniffed the air too.

"Yeah!"

"We're almost there." Alpha said.

He started to walk faster towards the nearby forest feeling energized. Getting carried away by their triumph, they weren't aware that they were not alone. Alpha then began to run until he came up upon a sight that nearly scared the two of them to death. They had entered into a bone graveyard. They were getting suspicious and frightened at the same time. Bones were scattered everywhere, and Alpha had to watch his step.

Then, the next thing they saw truly stunned them. Without any wind, the bones began to move! The bones suddenly started forming figures like the ones on Morph Island. Velociraptors! Except they were smaller and more agile. They were 3 feet tall and there were ten of them. It started out with five Raptors, but five more popped out from nearby Termite Mounds. Alpha tried to run away while Sheila held on, but there was a rocky hedge blocking their escape. Thankfully, Alpha spotted a suitable hole. Alpha told Sheila to carefully climb down his back. She slowly slid off of him. Once she reached the ground, Alpha morphed into Human form, quickly yanked her by the arm and ran for the hole. When he passed through the hole he morphed back into the Elephant and placed Sheila on his back again.

He looked back as the creatures were running towards the hole. He ran as fast as 15 mph, but the Raptors however, were right on him and one of them suddenly leaped and used its curved serrated teeth to bite Alpha's leg.

"RRRAAAAAOOOHH!! Alpha cried in pain. Then, another one jumped so high, it nearly took a bite out of Sheila, forcing her to hang onto Alpha's side with small, but sharp claws, causing more pain for Alpha.

"Sheila! Grab onto my trunk! Hurry!!" Sheila jumped and caught his trunk as a Raptor nearly had her in its jaws. Alpha placed her on one of his tusks, hoping that it'll protect her from harm.

He kept on running until they stopped at another rocky hedge. But this one was twice as big as the last one.

"Go! Hurry!" he told Sheila as he gave her a boost with his trunk to give her a head start. He then returned to Human form and looked back. The little carnivores were still ganging up on them. Alpha reached out his right arm, grabbed onto a ridge and started climbing. Never had they climbed a hedge as high as 120 feet in height, built with rocks and stones. Sheila looked back down to Alpha. It turned out, the Raptors could also climb!

"Climb faster!" she shouted. Alpha desperately climbed his way to catch up to her, but after all that he had been through, he felt as if he was getting weaker. But he was not going to give in. They had already climbed 60 feet, just half way to the top.

When Alpha found himself finally catching up to Sheila, he noticed that she stopped. The little dinosaurs were still determined to catch up regardless of the elevation.

"Hurry!" Alpha screamed to Sheila.

"I can't,—I can't do it anymore," she stammered

"Hang on Sheila, I'm coming!" he responded. Alpha rushed up to her. Once he finally reached her, she wasn't moving at all, just clinging onto the rocks.

"Sheila, listen to me!" he instructed. "We have to do this. There is no turning back. Let me help you. We can do this together. Trust me."

By those words, Sheila was finally convinced with a relieved smile. They began climbing side by side, outrunning the predators. Alpha and Sheila reached another ridge. But when Alpha looked back, Sheila slipped and slid half way down the hedge. Alpha slid after her and caught her by the arm as he kicked one of the little carnivores, causing it to plunge all the way down to the ground, shattering its hollow bones.

The two continued their climb. They desperately climbed and climbed and climbed for dear life. They then scaled up 110 feet . . . 113 feet . . . 116 feet . . . 118 feet, until they finally reached the top of the hedge while the Raptors unfortunately, were still behind them.

"Spirit of Queen Miriam," Alpha whispered in shock.

Sheila tried to follow his gaze. What she saw, filled her with astonishment. The view was unbelievable and a sign of hope. They had finally located the Forest environment.

"RRRAAHHHHHSSSS!!!" the Raptors hissed as they were right behind the couple.

"Sheila listen to me," Alpha instructed. "We have to jump." He suggested.

"But you are too weak to fly," she said. "Are you crazy?!" Sheila was getting more frightened as she didn't know what to do. "We'll be killed."

"And we'll be killed if we don't jump. It's the only way. It's worth the try."

"No, no, no, no I can't do this."

"Sheila, do you trust me?"

"What?

"Do you trust me?"

It took her a while to think about what to do, but she finally said "Yes."

They grabbed hands and jumped 120 feet down. The Raptors practically, had them in their jaws.

The two were still plunging down 120 feet. Alpha suddenly grabbed Sheila by the side and placed himself on top of her. Then he finally grew Gryphon wings out of his shoulders. He tried to catch some wind, but there was not enough. He desperately flapped his wings over and over, up and down, up and down, but it wasn't working. So Sheila had an idea and grew herself Gryphon wings also and they both flapped their wings at the same time. The plan worked, but it still wasn't enough to keep them stable. They tried pulling up, but instead flew right into the Forest. They tried so hard to keep themselves from hitting a tree. Unfortunately, there was a really gigantic mangrove tree in their path. They didn't have enough time to react, so Alpha's right wing hit the tree, causing the two to spin a full 360 degrees. The impact caused Alpha to let go of Sheila and he was the first to land violently on the forest ground. Then Sheila landed on Alpha's gut. At least they were both okay. They looked back at the huge hedge which actually looked as if it was a border between the Desert and Forest. The two spotted the Raptors as they stared down at them and then just simply vanished. Realizing that they had just survived the plunge of their lives, they started to laugh in relief.

Alpha and Sheila got up on their feet and brushed themselves with their hands to get the dirt off of them. Once they were done, they started their trail deep down into the forest. They instantly viewed the wonders of the environment; Flying lizards, rapid flower growth, color patterned birds, and even Termite Mounds. And what was different from Morph Island was that it didn't have a volcano.

"You know, I heard that every night, the whole forest glows in bright colors." He said. "Even small lizards can glow in the dark."

But as they were exploring, a male in Jaguar form ambushed them from the trees.

"Oh not again," they both complained.

Once again, they started running. But this time they had to find cover because this one had a bow and a case full of arrows. Suddenly, it sounded an alarm through the forest signaling more Morphers to come out from the bushes and trees. They really were security on patrol and surrounded the two with their arrows at the ready.

"Get behind me," Alpha instructed Sheila as he morphed into a Grizzly Bear.

Suddenly the Morphers began to disappear and appear. They were trying to confuse and stun him, just like the Raptors on Morph Island. Even Sheila was dazed. Sadly, Alpha was not quick to react when a Morpher connected a huge blow on the side of his head with a Bamboo stick.

The impact was so hard and so harsh, Alpha slowly passed out as he defenselessly watched the Morphers grab Sheila and take her away. Sheila desperately shouted at Alpha to help her, but Alpha had already lost consciousness.

CHAPTER 11

THE OPPORTUNITY

When Alpha woke up, he found himself in a cave with a male Morpher in Human form looking down at him. "OOHHHH!" Alpha moaned. "Where am I?" he asked.

"You're in the Valley," the Morpher said.

"The Forest Valley of Ambi?" Alpha asked in amazement, trying to sit up.

"Whoa, easy now boy."

"My head feels like I've been kicked by a Buffalo," he exaggerated as he felt a band made out of Caribou fur wrapped around his head.

"Ambi has a lot of unwelcoming creatures, huh?" the Morpher asked.

"Yeah, tons!"

"My name is Notch by the way," the Morpher introduced himself as he gave Alpha a coconut bowl of water. "And we have been expecting you, Alpha."

"How do you know my name?"

Notch then explained how he used to live with Alpha's family in their territory. And then, he disclosed something that shocked Alpha. For a short period, Notch raised Alpha and his brother Usrian after his parents died from the volcano eruption. Alpha was shocked to hear such news. He tried hard to remember that time but could not. He could only remember times playing with another morpher his age and not having his parents around to look out for him.

"Some story," Alpha said feeling sorry for what he had been through, but, he was astonished. Suddenly, a thought popped up in his mind. "Wait a minute!" "Where's Sheila?"

"Hmmm," Notch chuckled. "I was wondering when that was coming up. Don't worry. She's just enjoying the view. You should too."

Notch took Alpha's arm and helped him up to his feet. As he led Alpha to the opening, the sun was in his face blinding his view. But as he walked outside, he could see clearly, and the view was "breathtaking."

"Alpha, welcome to Ambi Valley," Notch presented.

Alpha was so astonished, his mouth dropped wide open. What he saw were pure green vegetation, six waterfalls falling down from the top of the Gorge leading to a lake and many creatures of the valley.

"WOOOOW!!" Alpha whispered. "This place looks richer than Morph Island."

Meanwhile, up above him, on his right was Sheila. She was standing on a ledge in Wolf form, enjoying the sights. Alpha was thankful she was alright.

"Alpha!" she called. "Up here!" He climbed up to her.

"Hey," he said. "I am so relieved that you're okay."

"You too," she said, morphing into Human form and giving him a hug. She then quickly turned back to the view again.

"Isn't this beautiful?" she asked.

"It is beautiful, especially the waterfalls." They even saw a family of morphers with well over one hundred members in the valley.

"This is like something beyond your wildest dreams," she described.

"Yeah," Alpha agreed. Then Sheila saw a long vine that was dangling on a tree above them.

"Come on, let's swing, shall we?" she suggested as she grabbed onto the vine.

Then, she swung off the ledge and was 19 feet above the lake until letting go of the vine and landing in the lake. Alpha thought to himself that this should make him feel better after what happened to his island. So he grabbed a vine of his own and swung.

"WHOOOOOOOOOUUU!!!" he shouted as he found himself over the land and over the lake. When he dropped into the lake, he made a big "WWHHUUSSHH!!!" splash. The two met underwater and started playing. They even caught salmon while they were underwater.

Later that day, the couple was still in the water, just relaxing. Eventually, they confessed that they both missed their evil siblings a little. But they were more joyful that they still had each other. As they looked at the sunset, Notch showed up with some members of the herd.

"So everything's going well I see," he pointed out.

"Oh yes, everything is fantastic!" Sheila complimented.

"Excellent," Notch said. "Well, listen Alpha." "The family members and I were purposing to offer you an opportunity."

"Oh really?" Alpha asked. "And what is this opportunity you speak of?"

Notch offered to give Alpha another opportunity to become king again by winning a contest. At first, Alpha refused to take the offer in order to have a civilized life with Sheila. But Sheila would rather be queen and have him be king. So she convinced him to accept and enter the contest. Notch became excited and notified him that he had already picked out his opponents. Notch then showed them to their den where a cozy nest, made out of leaf and soft twigs, was already set up.

Normally, Morph Island Morphers slept on their cave floors. They had grown accustomed to sleeping that way. When they saw the cozy nest with leaves and branches, they couldn't wait to try it out.

Night had fallen and the family was heading out. Meanwhile, Alpha and Sheila were just getting comfortable in their den. As they were lying down on their cozy nests, Alpha was worried about how the contest was going to be played out. Then he thought; as long as he had Sheila by his side, he knew that everything was going to be all right.

"Sheila, I just want you to know what a pleasure it is to have you with me because without you I am nothing.

"I know," she responded. Alpha looked at her as if that was an insult, but they both started to laugh.

"I love you Sheila," he said. Sheila looked at him in awe. "And I want us to be together, forever."

"So you saw my carvings about us being together huh?"

"Yes," he said. "But I also saved it."

He pulled the piece of the wall that Sheila carved on out of his arrow case. It still looked perfect, as it did back on the island. Sheila was very surprised that he actually saved the print.

"I love you too," she responded. Then Alpha kissed her on the head.

"Good night."

"Good night, my King."

She then leaned over to the other side while Alpha wrapped his arm around her waist and finally went to sleep.

Meanwhile, outside of the den, Notch and another Morpher went to check on the two. "Are you sure he could do this," the Morpher asked.

"Oh yes," Notch answered. "I am positively sure."

CHAPTER 12

THE CONTEST

Morning had slowly turned into afternoon, and everyone was already sitting on the Gorge as if they were on bleachers. Alpha was just escorted to his den that was on ground level. Once inside he was led to where he'd put on war paint. His three competitors were also in this area and they too were putting on their war paint. Their names were Saebr, the leader of the group, Tsurok, one of the Border guards, and Nook, the strongest Morpher in the Valley. They didn't seem to enjoy Alpha's presence. They just stared at him for a few moments with serious looks on their faces and went back to decorating themselves, using average sized glass as mirrors. Alpha was then led to a station where his painting materials were organized.

Thirty minutes had passed, and the herd was still waiting. Finally, a Morpher in Centaur form blew a horn made of bone, signaling that the contest was ready to begin. Meanwhile, Notch was on a ledge along with Sheila.

"Everyone!" he shouted. "We will now start the contest. But first, we shall meet our competitors. Our first three contenders are a group known as The Guardians. But let me remind you, there will only be one winner in this contest. First, the head of the group, give it up for Saebr!"

Saebr came out of the den and it was mostly the females who were screaming his name. But he winked at a female named Kayla, the one he wanted to be with. Kayla began to blush.

"Next, we have a Morpher who works as our Border Guard who can quickly coordinate an ambush on any trespasser. Everyone I give you Tsurok!"

Tsurok jogged out of the den and met up with Saebr with a high forearm greeting.

"Next is a Morpher filled with strength, power, and loves to show no mercy on a trespasser, Nook!" he introduced.

Nook stomped out of the den and met up with Saebr and Tsurok while the crowd was cheering his name.

"And now, for the special opponent." Notch continued. "The one who was once crowned King and ruled as the Last King of the beloved Morph Island and plans on winning his crown again. Ladies and gentlemorphers, I give you, Alphaaa!!"

Alpha walked out of the den slightly nervous, but as he heard Sheila shouting out his name he could feel his confidence increasing. Once he met up with the group, they still looked at him like he was the bad guy.

"Now, to make things more interesting, not only will the winner become King, he will automatically have a Queen." Notch explained. "And that lucky Queen to be, will be, Miss Sheila." Then everyone cheered in excitement.

"What?!" Sheila yelled.

"No!" Alpha shouted.

"What? No!" Saebr mumbled. He had planned to choose Kayla as his lovely Queen. "No, I don't want to win and have a Queen already chosen for me," he complained. "Especially her!" he sneered, insulting Sheila.

"Hey watch yourself!" Alpha snarled. Saebr stared at Alpha again and quickly walked up to him.

"You and your girlfriend shouldn't have come here in the first place," Saebr said with contempt.

"Silence!" Alpha demanded.

He suddenly swung with a right hook, but Saebr was swift to dodge and shoved him to the ground. Alpha was able to flip him over. They both got up at the same time. Saebr then pounced on Alpha. But Alpha grabbed his throat and threw him down to the ground with force. But Saebr grew a long tail and swept Alpha's legs, causing him to fall on his back.

Meanwhile Sheila was complaining to Notch. "You can't allow this," she shouted.

"Apologies Ms.," Notch said. "But I am confident that Alpha will fulfill the prophecy by winning this brutal contest and becoming our first King and having his desired Queen."

"Brutal!" Sheila exclaimed. "What do you mean brutal?"

Notch let out a low chuckle. As he turned back to the battle, Saebr had Alpha's leg in his jaws. Tsurok and Nook finally broke up the fight and regrouped. The three lined up in front of Alpha posing a threat to him. Alpha had no choice, but to back down. Notch then shouted and said that the objective of this challenge was to climb the 60 foot Gorge and grab a Golden staff. But the obstacles were very challenging. The obstacles included falling logs and boulders. A referee showed up and explained the rules that included no flying to the top of the Gorge and no use of teamwork effort; it's every man for himself.

Just as Sheila couldn't take any of this anymore, she flew down to Alpha.

"Alpha, you don't have to do this," she said as she feared that he would lose the game and someone else would win her.

"No, no. I have to do this," he replied. "I have to complete the prophecy. Hey, it's going to be alright." "Trust me." Those words had cheered her up a little bit. It was enough for her to kiss him on the cheek.

"Good luck," she said as she flew back on the ledge where Notch was still standing.

"Contestants, on your mark," the referee called out. "Get set!" Then he blew Dragon fire out of his mouth, signaling "Go."

The four sprinted to the Gorge and started climbing. In human form, they desperately reached for the nearest ledge they could grab on to. Alpha was climbing like he was still running from the volcano eruption. While they were still scaling up the Gorge, they could see the staff high in plain sight, but then suddenly, large boulders and logs started rolling down the Gorge. A boulder was heading towards Alpha. Luckily, he leaped over it. But when he landed, he slipped and slid halfway down the Gorge. Fortunately, he caught himself on a ledge and continued to climb. With all of his might, Alpha rapidly passed the three Guardians and was on his way to victory. But Tsurok wasn't going to allow it. Unexpectedly, carelessly, he morphed into a Falcon. He hastily flew to Alpha. When he finally caught up, he used his beak and started pecking him, giving his two friends a chance to go on. But luckily, the referee spotted him in bird form, assuming he was going to fly up the Gorge even though one of the rules were "no flying." He made a call and had no choice but to disqualify him. But Tsurok paid no attention and continued his assault on Alpha.

Then Alpha saw an extensive log falling towards them giving him an idea. He grew Dragon wings and flapped them at Tsurok. This caused Tsurok to catch lots of wind while standing right in the log's way. Next thing Tsurok felt the impact of the log crashing into him.

"Thank you Usarian," Alpha said remembering that move from his brother during the fight they had.

He continued climbing and caught up with the other two. He was trying to go after Saebr, but Nook caught him dead in his tracks and yanked Alpha by the hair.

"AAAARRHHH!!!" he cried.

"Where do you think you're going, Former King?!" he asked in a bullying tone.

He then threw Alpha halfway across the Gorge and he landed with a loud thud. Sheila was standing on the left side of the competition area. While watching nervously at her King-to-be, she still had confidence in him.

Meanwhile, Alpha was trying to take down Nook, but it was really Nook who was taking down Alpha. He kept on pounding him with his huge Gorilla formed fists. But Alpha then came up with another idea. He cornered himself. Nook was not familiar with this plan of his as he lifted up his right fist to finish him off. Suddenly, he swung, but he missed and instead punched the wall with force. Because of that, the wall started to vibrate, causing some small to huge rocks to tumble down towards them. When Nook looked up, Alpha grabbed and shoved him hitting the back of Nook's head against the wall. Nook was dazed and stunned. He looked up just in time to see boulders dog piling on him. The crowd was shocked that Nook didn't make it out of the pile.

"Sorry big guy," Alpha mumbled to himself as he continued on his climb.

Sheila, on the other hand, was approached by some female Morphers and Kayla.

"So are you nervous about someone else being your King instead of Alpha?" one of the females asked.

"No I'm not," Sheila answered. "Because I know that Alpha will win the challenge and we will live happily with our lives as the royal King and Queen."

"But what if Alpha doesn't win?" Kayla asked jealously for she too wanted to have a romantic life with Saebr as King and Queen.

"He will win," Sheila said confidently. "You'll see." "He will win."

Back at the Gorge, the game was now left with two competitors. Alpha had finally caught up to Saebr who was about 6 feet away from the Staff. As he saw Alpha catching up, he was getting a little discouraged, but he still had some confidence.

"So you think that you have the advantage by leaving me alone to fend for myself huh?" Saebr mumbled to himself. "Well let's see about that!" he said as he leaped off the wall and pounced on Alpha.

Alpha knew that Saebr wasn't going down easily without a violent fight. He tried to weaken Alpha by biting, clawing and shoving him into the wall, but Alpha wouldn't give in. Alpha then punched him on his right jaw, causing Saebr to stumble and fall on his stomach. As he spotted Alpha who was about to climb, he kicked some dirt in his face. Once he realized that Alpha couldn't see, Saebr grew an Iguanodon tail and swung at his mid section, causing him to fall 3 feet down. Saebr then got back up and started climbing again.

Sheila put her hand over her mouth, devastated by what had just happened.

Alpha finally recovered from the fall and continued his pursuit on Saebr. He didn't feel like wasting time to fight him anymore. So instead, once he reached him, he leaped on top of Saebr's shoulders and jumped to a higher ledge. Amazingly, he managed to reach the top of the Gorge where the Staff was standing right in front of his eyes.

But before he could reach for the Staff, Saebr grabbed on to his ankle and held it. Alpha desperately reached out his hand for the Staff while hanging on to the ledge. Saebr stood with his left foot, on one of the logs that was slanted between two ledges and his raptor foot claws sunk into the log. Alpha then tried kicking him with both of his feet, but it didn't work. He even tried batting him with a hard tail, but that also didn't work.

As Alpha got closer to the prize, there was too much movement for the log, and also for the ledges. It kept rolling back and forth and one of the ledges made a cracking noise. It could no longer support the weight and movement of the log and the ledge gave way, causing the log to fall. Saebr's foot claws were still caught in the log and he was still hanging on to Alpha. Luckily, Alpha still managed to hang on and reach for the Staff.

But then, there was a loud cracking noise coming from the ledge that Alpha was clinging onto. It couldn't support the weight of Alpha, Saebr and the log, so that also gave way, causing both competitors to plunge down the Gorge.

"NOOOO!!!" Sheila screamed as she watched Alpha falling viciously down the little mountain along with some rocks and logs.

Saebr's claw was still latched into the log which suddenly started rolling on him. Meanwhile, Tsurok gained consciousness. He met up with Nook, who also came to and managed to free himself from the boulder pile. They suddenly felt the Gorge shaking.

"You feel that?" Tsurok asked. When they finally looked up, the expressions on their faces turned from relief to awe. They couldn't believe that more rocks were falling and heading straight towards them as if it was an avalanche.

"Oh no," they said at the same time. "Not again."

When they finally tried to make a run for it, the rocks had swept them up like a tidal wave. Soon after, the whole side of the Gorge was coated with rocks and boulders.

Sheila, her fellow female friends and Notch flew down to the ground. What they saw, was horrifying. Nothing but rocks and debris. No sign of life anywhere. But thankfully, Tsurok, Nook and Saebr who freed his foot during the fall, made it out of the pile and flew off the Gorge with some bruises. Notch looked up at the top of the mountain, but couldn't see the Staff.

"Where's the Staff?" he asked.

"Where's Alpha?" Sheila asked, changing the subject. Everyone including Sheila looked at the Gorge, hoping that Alpha made it.

"Come on old friend," Notch pleaded.

Sheila was praying to herself that she would see her King. Then suddenly, a hand popped out of the rocks. It was clear that Alpha survived the impact. Once he came out of the pile, everyone could see the Golden Staff in his hand. He got onto his feet and stood majestically on the rocks with the staff glowing brightly. Sheila gazed up in relief. Alpha grew wings and flew off the Gorge and landed on the ground. Sheila sprinted towards Alpha and gave him a tight hug.

"I knew you would win," Sheila said as she hugged him.

Clouds had suddenly formed over the island and rain started to fall. Then, all the Morphers on the ground and on the Gorge began bowing their heads as they prepared to worship their first King.

CHAPTER 13

ALPHA ASCENDS

As Alpha watched the heads bowing to him, he heard beating noises on the Gorge. It was Notch (mysteriously back on the mountain) who was signaling Alpha to make himself noticeable on this long 5 foot ledge they call The Royal Ledge. Alpha obeyed the command and made his way to the Gorge. While he was heading towards it, he caught his three competitors bowing their heads.

"Good game boys," he complimented.

"All the same to you, my King," Saebr replied breathing heavily.

"I have to say," Alpha commented. "I admire your skills and techniques."

He then gave them a high forearm salute and the three bowed their heads again. Alpha then made it up to the Gorge, climbing 40 feet using the Golden Staff to help him ascend to where Notch was standing, and also bowing his head. Alpha then smiled at Notch for believing in him and felt the urge to give him a hug.

"Fulfill the prophecy, old friend," Notch said.

He grabbed the staff out of Alpha's hand and bowed his head again. Alpha nervously, but majestically walked along the Royal Ledge. Once he got to the end of the Ledge, he saw a stone carving of a crown that magically glowed in shiny gold. Then something mysterious happened. Alpha could still see the rain falling, but couldn't feel the rain drops on his body. When he looked up at the sky, he saw the rain clouds separating, revealing a clear night sky with stars. He then heard a warm, soft voice through the sky that happened to be the voice of his mother, Miriam.

"Your destiny, begins now," she said in a wise tone.

Alpha closed his eyes, feeling his body relax at last and put his head down. Then he ascended with a screech of the mighty Postosuchus.

"AAARRRRAAAGGGHHH!!!" Then he let out a Raptor howl, "AAAYYYYGAAA!!!" And then let out a thunderous Lion roar, "HHAAAGGRRR!!!" Lastly, he let out a T-Rex growl, "AAAAGAAAA!!!" Thunder echoed loudly through the skies along with bright lightning. The Morphers raised their heads and hands and then bowed to their king again.

CHAPTER 14

A WHOLE NEW LIFE, A WHOLE NEW BEGINNING

The next day, Alpha began to dress for the ceremony. As King, he wore a Lion's fur as a cape, Eagle's feather for neckwear, three golden bracelets on each of his arms, and primary color paintings on his face and chest. Once he was all set, he heard a Morpher at the mouth of the den introduce his Queen, Sheila. When she came inside the den, she was glowing! She was dressed in a purple, silky gown, with sparkles that lit up and surrounded her face in an angel-like radiance, silver necklace, two earrings made out of Parrot feathers, a Peacock's feather on her head, and make up.

"Wow!" Alpha said. "You look beautiful, my Queen." He complimented as he bowed to her.

"And all the same to you, my King," she bowed in gratitude. "I'm sure your mother is proud of you."

"No," Alpha replied. "She is proud of *us*." They then hugged each other in joy.

"Uh, I'm sorry to interrupt Your Majesties, but everyone is waiting," Notch's voice broke the spell.

"Thank you Notch," Alpha said.

"Are you ready?" Sheila asked.

"Let's do this," Alpha responded with confidence. "Are you ready?" he asked turning to Sheila.

"Let's do this," she repeated.

As they walked to the cave opening, Notch looked so proud. He had never looked this way in life until this day.

"Your Majesties, Ambi Island awaits," he said as he bowed his head and stretched his arm to the opening. The King and the Queen responded by bowing their heads back in gratitude.

As the couple walked out into the Open, and through the sunlight, the Valley rumbled with cheers. The two walked along the Royal Ledge. Once they got to the end of the Ledge, the Morphers then bowed their heads and the Valley immediately got quiet. Then Notch came from behind with the royal crowns and Alpha's Golden Staff. He gave the Staff to Alpha and put the crown which was gold, designed with teeth carvings, and Emeralds on top of his head. Then, he put a silver crown that was designed with silver leaf carvings, diamonds and purple stones on Sheila's head.

"My fellow Morphers," Notch called. "Warriors, securities, parents, children and elders; It is my pleasure, my honor, to announce our salvation. I give you King Alpha and Queen Sheila!"

Once he threw their hands up in the air, the valley rumbled in cheers once again in different ways. Horses neighed along with some zebras, antelopes hopped, Wolfs howled, the big cats such as leopards and jaguars growled, monkeys chattered, clapped and pounded on the rocks, Elephants stomped in the water and trumpeted and birds flew freely across the skies. Alpha and Sheila felt overjoyed just by looking at the crowd. Then for show, Alpha raised his Golden Staff in the air. But then, he felt a ray of sun light shining down on him. He then heard his mother's voice again.

"I am so proud of you, my son," she said. "Well done."

Alpha smiled and closed his eyes as he felt a soft breeze blowing leaves at his face. The leaves were actually his mother's hands touching his face. She also blew leaves at Sheila, for she was proud of her as well. The two then turned to each other.

"They did a very nice job with these crowns huh?" Alpha asked.

"Yes," she replied. "They are beautiful."

"Not as beautiful as you are," he said with a soft voice.

Sheila smiled her crystal looking eyes at him. Alpha smiled back at her. Then, he placed his hand on the right side of her face. They suddenly felt their heads leaning towards each other and they touched. They were kissing! What they felt, was magical. Miriam then made the flying leaves circle around them. They felt so free, that they didn't stop. The Morphers once again continued their worshiping calls.

Meanwhile, Notch nodded in joy as he gazed at the crowd. Then he looked up at the skies knowing that life on Ambi Island, will never be the same again!!!